GW00730568

Awesome George Save

Dan Colegate, Esther Dingley & Kim Prior

www.estheranddan.com

Awesome George wanted to play

while all his sisters slept one day,

so he tried to pass the time alone

by chewing on his soft toy bone.

"This bone tastes good, but it's not as fun

as going outside to chase and run",

thought George as he sat and looked around,

when all of a sudden he heard a sound.

A banging, clanging, scary knocking,

which to other pups might have been quite shocking,

but brave young George saw it was nothing more,

than the wind blowing open the kitchen door.

Well, George was never one to miss,

a chance to have some fun like this,

and so leaving his snoozing sisters behind

he stretched his legs and strolled outside.

And the first thing that he noticed there

was the humans in their garden chair,

dozing and dreaming and snoring so loud,

she was noisier than a football crowd!

which is probably why they couldn't hear,

as Awesome George sneaked ever so near,

through their chair legs and continued past

into the long, long garden grass.

"Well, this is a grand adventure for sure"

thought Awesome George as he explored,

leaving the house far, far behind

to see what games and fun he'd find.

First he found a lot of sticks,

which he quickly chewed into smaller bits,

and then he surprised a wriggling worm

that was digging near an old milk churn.

For a while he chased a butterfly,

but eventually it got too high,

so instead he decided he would dig

an enormous hole, both deep and big.

But just as he was about to start

to push the grass and soil apart,

he heard a frightened, small voice cry,

"I've hurt my wing and cannot fly".

And George, not sure if he'd really heard,

looked up to see a baby bird

flapping on a nearby mound,

unable to get up off the ground.

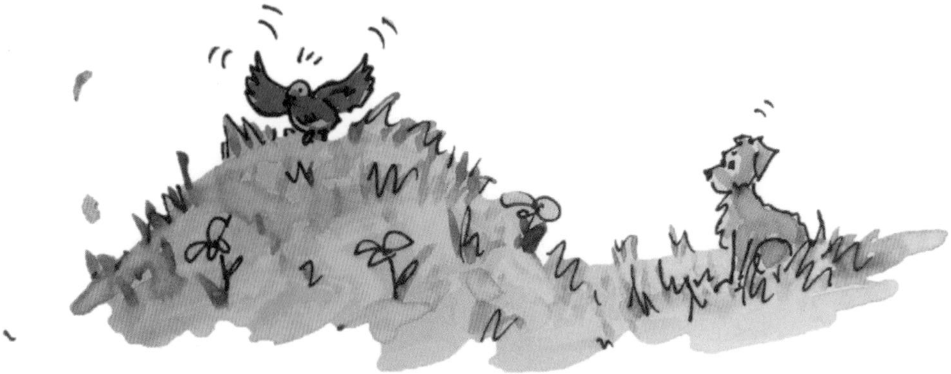

"Don't be afraid, I'll be there quick"

called George to the young, frightened chick,

and with that he began to bound

to join the bird upon the mound.

"What happened here, what can I do?"

said George to the little scared cuckoo.

"Well, I fell out of the nest you see,

and banged my wing upon this tree."

"And now, until my mum gets home

I have to wait here all alone,

and I'm really scared, as scared as can be

that the cat is going to come after me."

"I'm Awesome George, I have no fear,

I'll make sure there's no cat near here."

And with that George set right about

keeping watch and looking out.

And hiding quietly behind the tree,

sure enough, he could soon see

a cat's tail flicking up nearby,

so barking out a warning cry

He charged across the grassy floor

towards the tail, barking more,

he scared the hungry cat away.

It wouldn't scare the chick that day!

A while later they heard the sound

of bigger wings flapping to the ground.

"Oh there you are" said the chick's scared mum

"all alone in the hot, hot sun."

"Well, actually I'm safe you see,

because Awesome George looked after me."

"Oh, thank you George" exclaimed the mum,

"without you that cat would've surely come".

And George's chest swelled up with pride,

he felt so brave and strong inside.

"Time to head home and tell the pack,

they'll be excited to see me when I'm back".

"Oh, George, where have you ever been?"

said his sisters as he crept back in.

"Up to no good I bet" said one,

"he's always in trouble when he's gone".

And so George decided not to say

just how brave he'd been that day,

because it didn't matter if his sister knew,

so he settled down for a quiet chew.

THE END

THE REAL GEORGE'S STORY

These joy filled stories have been inspired by incredible true events. In 2017, Dan and Esther crossed paths with a little ginger and white stray dog on the Southern Coast of Spain.

3 years earlier Dan had been rushed into emergency surgery and the couple were told to say "a proper goodbye, just in case". Dan did eventually recover and it kickstarted a search for a new way of life as the couple drove away from their lives in Durham in a second-hand campervan.

It was during their travels that they came across the little dog, who had been abandoned with no collar or chip, and who had been found sheltering during a huge storm by a lady called Blanca. There is a huge problem of dogs being abandoned in Spain, where dogs often get driven out to rural villages and left there.

Esther and Dan decided the campervan had room for one more. They named her Leela and instantly they became a very contented travelling trio. But bedraggled and very skinny little Leela was hiding a big surprise. Two weeks later, Bella, George, Rose, Pati, Teddy and Jess arrived! Dan and Esther committed to raising them and finding them good homes.

Whilst Teddy and Jess found their new homes with some amazing friends, for one reason or another, Bella, George, Pati and Rose stayed and joined the travelling team for the next 3 years. Both humans and all five dogs enjoyed incredible adventures as they travelled through Europe, mostly in the campervan but sometimes house-sitting.

From the beautiful sandy beaches of Spain, to chasing butterflies through sunflower fields in rural France, to riding cable cars up into the snowy mountains of Switzerland, they spread smiles (and a lot of woofs) wherever they went! Bella and Rose even took Esther for a very long, 27 day dog walk across the French Pyrenean mountains... But that's a whole other adventure story!

Dan wrote the first of these stories (Awesome George Saves The Day) as a gift for Esther when the pups were just a few months old and they were house-sitting in France. As the pups grew, it was wonderful to watch them play as a family but also watch their individual characters developing, which Dan captures in these stories.

During their travels Dan and Esther experienced so much kindness from complete strangers that it changed their whole worldview. From this kindness and also from the absolute love and joy the dogs radiated, Dan, a former scientific academic, drew inspiration and creativity.

It was always Esther's dream to one day see these stories being read to children but neither she nor Dan could draw. 3 years on and during the COVID19 lockdowns in April 2020, Esther, Dan and the dogs found themselves back at the same housesit where the pups had grown up. Determined to see her dream come true, Esther used the extra time to reach out for help.

It was the wonderfully kind and talented, retired PE teacher, Kim Prior who answered the call. Thanks to her beautiful illustrations it has been possible to bring these stories to life.

Our hope is that both children and adults enjoy and benefit from these stories. The cost has been kept as low as possible so that they have the potential to reach and make smile as many children as possible. Any small proceeds go to topping up the dogs "bone" accounts!

So thank you and woof woof for purchasing this book .....
Leela, Bella, Rose, Pati & George

You can read more about the dogs and see their individual profiles at:

http://www.estheranddan.com/p/meettheteam

You can read about Esther and Dan's full story in the book **"What Adventures Shall We Have Today?"**, in which Dan captures the very best travel tales from 6 years on the road. Naturally the dogs are the stars of half of this book, which is also available on Amazon.

Dan's inspiration also led to the creation of another collection of heart-warming and emotional dog poems, which combined with pictures, is a great gift for dog lovers of any age and guaranteed to bring joy, laughter and maybe even a tear or two.

"Love, Fluff and Chasing Butterflies" is also available on Amazon as an eBook and paperback and 50% of the royalties are donated to the Dogs Trust.

OTHER BOOKS BY DAN, ESTHER & KIM

Puppy Pack Adventures (The Complete Collection)

Bounding Bella Spreads A Smile

Awesome George Saves The Day

Lovely Leela Finds A Family

Clever Rose And The Mucky Beach

Great Uncle Dan And His Zoo In A Van*

(*Raising Funds for Rainbows Hospice For Children

& Young People)

Great Uncle Dan

& His Zoo In A Van

Dan Colegate , Esther Dingley & Kim Prior

Printed in Great Britain
by Amazon